Written by Shaun Brown

THIS BOOK BELONGS TO

_____

This is Eloise! She loves her green bag!

This is Eloise's New Teacher! Mrs Brown

This is Rosie! This is Eloise's new best friend.

Mom in her car

Join Eloise on her first week at school!
Eloise is a smart little girl who is nervous about starting a new school.

Eloise was excited for her first day of school.

She picked out her favorite dress and put on her shoes.

Her mom drove her to school and they said goodbye.

Eloise nervously entered the classroom and found a seat.

The teacher welcomed her and introduced her to the class.

Everyone smiled and said hi. Eloise felt relieved.

During the day, Eloise made a new best friend Rosie, and learned a lot.

She was excited to go back the next day and explore more.

The second day was filled with laughter and fun.

Eloise was getting more comfortable and confident.

She made more friends and joined in on activities.

On the third day, Eloise found her place in the school.

She shared her talents and passions with her new friends.

The fourth day was a special day for Eloise.

She made a presentation in front of the entire class.

Everyone clapped and cheered for her. Eloise was proud.

The fifth day was a field trip to the museum.

At the weekend, Eloise had a special project to work on.

She put her creative energy to work and made something amazing.

Sunday was the last day of the week.

Eloise had made lots of friends and learned so much.

She thought about all her new friends she had made at school.

Eloise was proud of all she had accomplished in her first week.

She was excited to come back the next week and continue learning.

Eloise was ready for the challenges and adventures ahead.

She was ready to take on the world and follow her dreams.

Eloise was ready for what the future held.

She was ready to take on each new day with enthusiasm and courage.

Eloise was ready to make the most of every week of school.

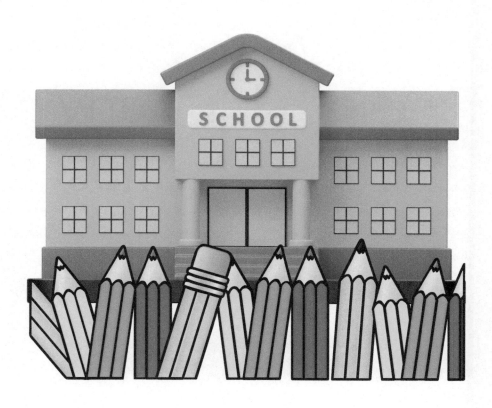

SPOT THE DIFFERENCE!

CAN YOU FIND ALL 10?

Time to think back!

1. What is the name of Eloise's new Best Friend?
2. What colour is Moms Car?
3. What did Eloise do on day 5?
4. What colour is Eloise's Bag?
5. What was the 2nd day filled with?

WHAT DO YOU THINK?

Written by Shaun Brown

Designed by pikisuperstar /
Freepik & Shaun Brown

S.B BOOKS

SPOT THE DIFFERENCE!

ANSWERS!

Time to think back!

1. **Rosie**
2. **Red**
3. **Go to the Museum**
4. **Green**
5. **Laughter and Fun**

Hope you enjoyed Eloise's first week at school!

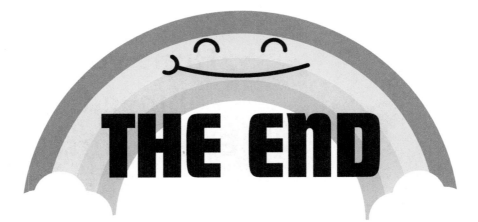

Written by Shaun Brown

Designed by pikisuperstar /
Freepik & Shaun Brown

S.B BOOKS

Printed in Great Britain
by Amazon

29397993R00044